Bad Cat

puts on his top hat

by Tracy-Lee McGuinness-Kelly

 LITTLE, BROWN AND COMPANY

New York ❧ Boston

Also by Tracy-Lee McGuinness-Kelly:

Bad Cat

Little, Brown and Company

Time Warner Book Group
1271 Avenue of the Americas, New York, NY 10020
Visit our Web site at www.lb-kids.com

First Edition

Library of Congress Cataloging-in-Publication Data

McGuinness, Tracy.
Bad Cat puts on his top hat / by Tracy-Lee McGuinness-Kelly.—1st ed.
p. cm. — (Bad Cat)
Summary: Bad Cat has a variety of adventures in the city he lives in, which he calls the Big Stinky.
ISBN 0-316-60547-6
[1. Cats—Fiction. 2. City and town life—Fiction.] I. Title.
PZ7.M478563Baf 2005
[E]—dc22
2003022031

10 9 8 7 6 5 4 3 2 1

TWP

Printed in Singapore

The illustrations for this book were done in Photoshop on a Mac.
The text was set in Sabon, and the display type was created by the artist.

Dedicated to and for
the child in all of us

yummy
yummy
yum
yum!

Bad Cat lived in a huge, dirty city. He called it the Big Stinky. The sun had just risen in the Big Stinky, and Bad Cat's tummy was rumbling. Boy, was he hungry!

Bad Cat noticed an open kitchen door and slipped inside. He put on a chef's hat and started frying eggs and squirting jelly on toast.

Suddenly a scratchy voice yelled, "Hey, you, bad cat! Who said you could do that?" Mr. Sausagefingers, the restaurant cook, came from the back and he looked boiling mad! Bad Cat flung his egg whisk up in the air and slid across the floor as fast as he could.

Mr. Sausagefingers began scrubbing the counter when he noticed a delicious smell coming from the stove. People were lining up outside the restaurant, dying to try a bite! "Come back!" he called. "Your food smells so yummy and now I have a big line of customers!"

But Bad Cat had already run down the street.

"I'm a bad cat, bad cat, cooking eggy yolks, flipping up the pancakes, cracking funny jokes!"

Bad Cat stopped running when he saw a bright yellow ball. He kicked the ball, and it bounced off of a big boy's head.

"Hey, you, bad cat! No one dares to do that!" It was Billy Bashface,
a mean bully who had taken the ball from some little kids. Bad Cat
took off without looking back.

Billy saw the little kids smiling and laughing now that they had their ball back. He realized how awful he'd been. "Don't go!" he cried. "You've helped me see that being a bully makes me unhappy!"

But Bad Cat was long gone.

"I'm a bad cat, brave cat,

nothing scares me now,
not even bullies,

BIFF,
BAM,
POW!"

Bad Cat slowed down when he saw an artist staring out the window of a studio. He went inside, dipped his paws in paint, and pressed them onto an empty canvas.

Suddenly a high-pitched voice squeaked, "Hey, you, bad cat! Don't you touch that!" It was Millicent Moneybags, the owner of the studio, and her face was purple with anger. Bad Cat flew down the steps.

Then Millicent saw her artist's eyes begin to sparkle. He picked up his painting tools and began furiously working away. "Come back!" she yelped. "You've inspired my artist to create!"

But Bad Cat was already on his way.

"I'm a bad cat, art cat, squiggly lines and blobs, splotches, dots, and scribbles, paint thrown on in globs!"

Bad Cat stopped on the street when he noticed a ladder being lowered from a high window.

He began climbing the ladder and bumped right into two men carrying big bundles on their way down.

Ooooh, what a sight! Hands gripped, the ladder slipped, balance was lost, objects got tossed, bodies flipped, pants got ripped, vases smashed, cameras flashed, jewels fell out, and people did shout, "Look out! Look out!"

Everyone saw a big bag of jewels sitting at Bad Cat's feet. "Hey, you, bad cat! It's shocking you took that!" Bad Cat shook his head. He wanted to explain that he didn't take the jewels, but before he could say anything, the crowd surrounded him.

Then a voice shouted out, "Wait! Isn't that Harry Hairyhands and Teddy Fatcheeks, the famous jewel robbers?"

Everyone looked and agreed that indeed it was. They immediately let go of Bad Cat and nabbed Harry and Teddy.

Bad Cat was lifted up onto the ladder and they all cheered.

"Bad Cat, Bad Cat,
There's a big reward for doing that!"

Millicent Moneybags threw a fancy dessert party to celebrate Bad Cat's recovery of the stolen jewels. Everyone stuffed themselves with scrumptious sweets and drank lots of fizzy pop. Bad Cat sang for the crowd.

"I'm a bad cat, bad cat,
jelly wobble joy,
sticky buns and cupcakes,
gooey pie, oh boy!"

When most of the goodies
had been gobbled, Bad Cat
was ready to leave. He licked a
little blob of cream off the end of
his nose, waved good-nightie-noodles,
and wished everyone sweet dreams.

Bad Cat stopped when he heard music coming from a backstage door. He tiptoed inside. As soon as he got in, a top hat was placed on his head and he was swept up onto a brightly lit stage.

Suddenly a commanding voice blared, "Hey, you, bad cat! That's not your hat!" It was Baxter Bunnyteeth, the famous director, and he wasn't at all pleased. Bad Cat quickly tap-danced off behind the curtain and vanished.

Baxter was huffing and puffing to himself when he noticed all of his performers were doing the Bad Cat boogie. It was truly sensational!
"Come back!" he pleaded. "You've razzle-dazzled my dancers! I want you to star in my next show!"

But Bad Cat was way off in the distance.

"I'm Bad Cat, top hat cat,
dancing on my way,
to the twinkly lights
in stinkytown,
razzle-dazzle hey!"